A NOTE ABOUT THE TEXT

The song we know today as "Over the River and Through the Wood" is adapted from a poem by Lydia Maria Child. The poem was first published in her popular three-volume anthology for boys and girls, *Flowers for Children* (1844–1846). During the nineteenth century it was reprinted many times under various titles. Child's poem became the unofficial anthem of Thanksgiving after her friend John Greenleaf Whittier included it in *Child Life* (1871), his immensely popular collection of nineteenth-century children's verse. The original poem was twelve verses long, but it has often been shortened to six. This book uses the six verses that appeared in the Whittier anthology under the title "Thanksgiving Day."

Published in the United States by North-South Books Inc., New York 10001.
Published simultaneously in Great Britain, Canada, Australia, and New Zealand in 1993 by North-South Books Inc., an imprint of NordSüd Verlag AG, CH-8005 Zürich, Switzerland.
First paperback edition published in 1998.

Library of Congress Cataloging-in-Publication Data
Child, Lydia Maria Francis, 1802–1880.
[Boy's Thanksgiving Day]
Over the river and through the wood; a Thanksgiving
poem / by Lydia Maria Child; illustrated with woodcuts by Christopher Manson.
Originally published in v. 2 of the author's Flowers for children, 1884,
Under the title: A boy's Thanksgiving Day.
Summary: Scenes from rural New England illustrate this familiar poem, that became a well-known song, about a Thanksgiving Day visit to Grandmother's house.
Thanksgiving Day—Juvenile poetry. 2. Children's poetry, American. 3. Children's Songs—Texts. [1.Thanksgiving Day—Poetry. 2.Songs.] I. Manson, Christopher, ill.
II. Title. PS1293.B68 1993
811'.3—dc20 93-16614

A CIP catalogue record for this book is available from The British Library.

The illustrations are woodcuts painted with watercolor.
Musical arrangement and typesetting by Perry Iannone.
The text and display type is set in Adobe Caslon.
Typography by Marc Cheshire.

Printed in China by Toppan Leefung Packaging & Printing (Dongguan) Co., Ltd., Dongguan, P.R.C., July 2010.

ISBN: 978-1-55858-959-9 (PAPERBACK)
7 9 PB 10 8

www.northsouth.com

Over the River and Through the Wood

A Thanksgiving Poem by Lydia Maria Child

ILLUSTRATED WITH WOODCUTS BY

Christopher Manson

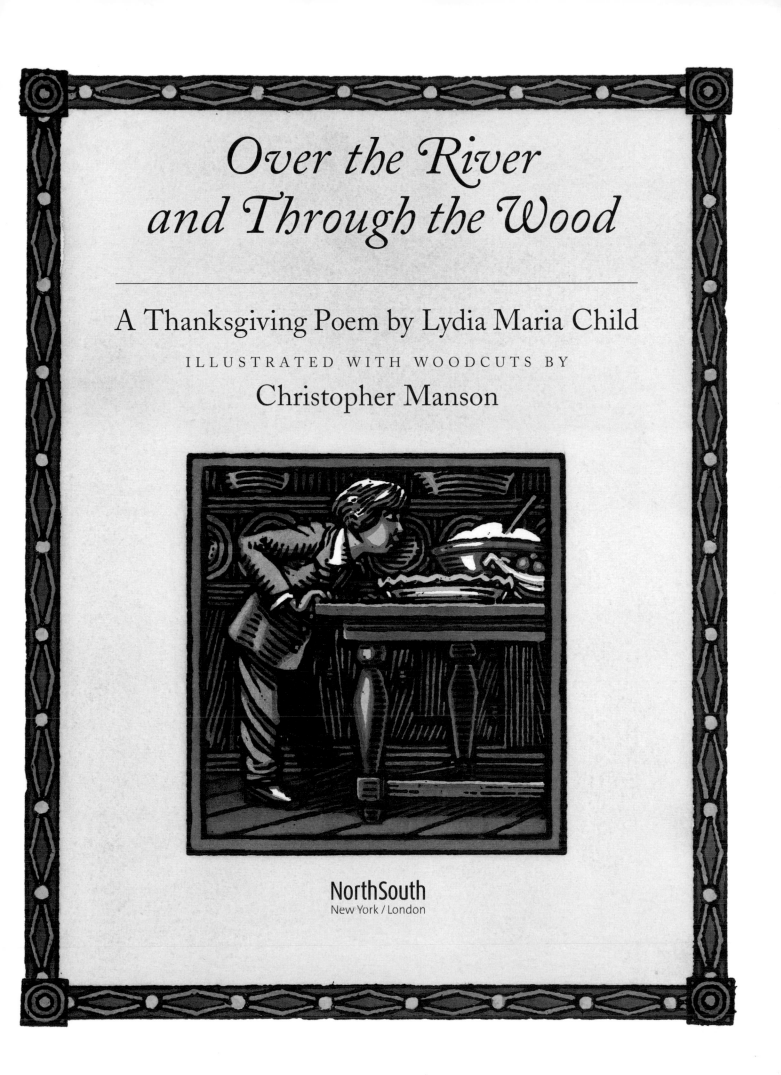

NorthSouth
New York / London

Over the river and through the wood,
To Grandfather's house we go;

The horse knows the way
To carry the sleigh
Through the white and drifted snow.

Over the river and through the wood—
Oh, how the wind does blow!

It stings the toes
And bites the nose,
As over the ground we go.

Over the river and through the wood,
To have a first-rate play.

Hear the bells ring,
"Ting-a-ling-ding!"
Hurrah for Thanksgiving Day!

Over the river and through the wood,
Trot fast, my dapple-gray!

Spring over the ground
Like a hunting hound!
For this is Thanksgiving Day.

Over the river and through the wood,
And straight through the barnyard gate.

We seem to go
Extremely slow—
It is so hard to wait!

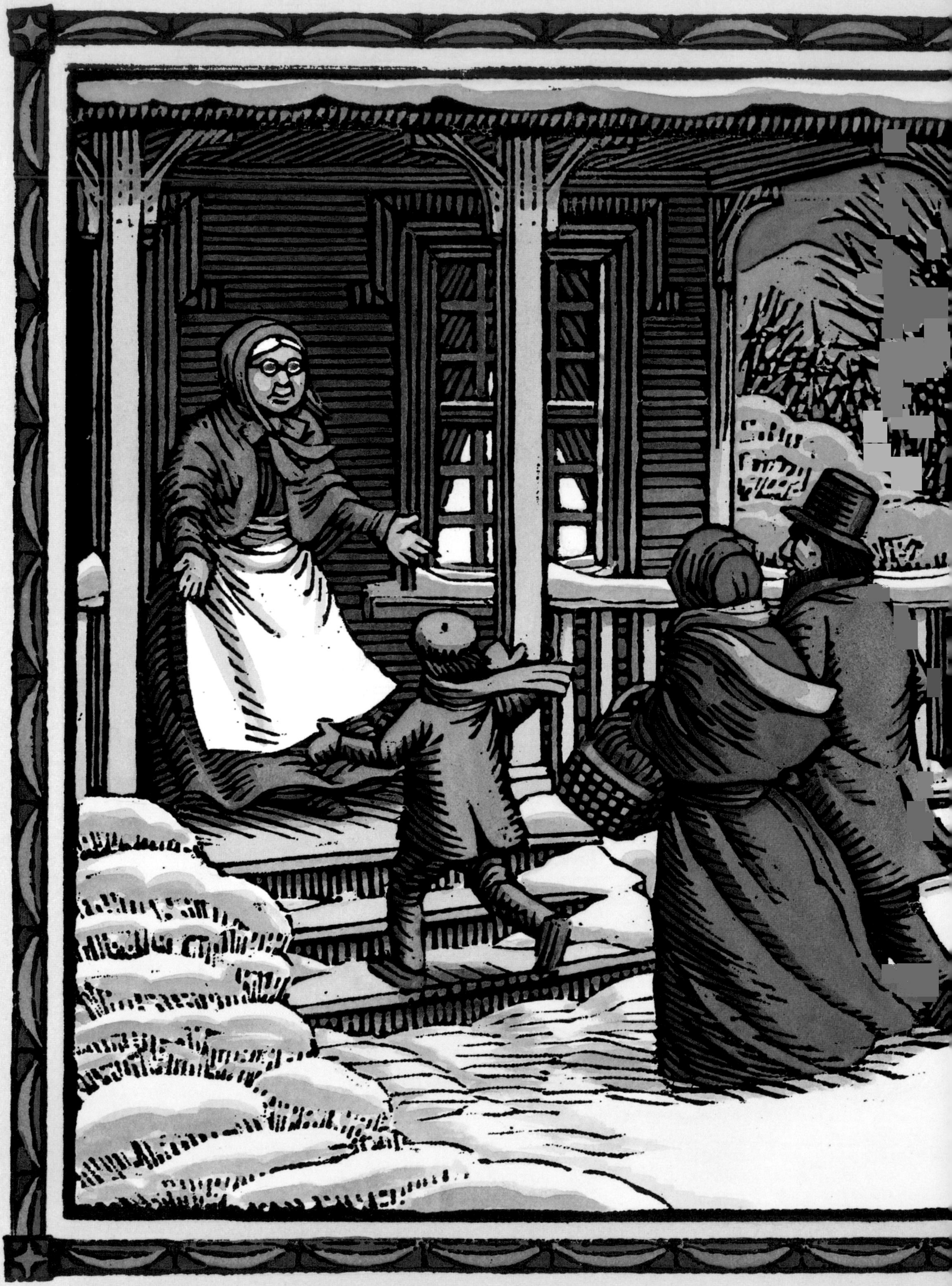

Over the river and through the wood—
Now Grandmother's cap I spy!

Hurrah for the fun!
Is the pudding done?
Hurrah for the pumpkin pie!

Allegro

Lydia Maria Child

1. O - ver the riv - er and through the wood, To Grand-fa-ther's house we go; _____ The horse knows the way To car - ry the sleigh Through the white and drift - ed snow. _____ O - ver the riv - er and through the wood— Oh, how the wind does blow! _____ It stings the toes And bites the nose, As o - ver the ground we go. _____

2. Over the river and through the wood,
   To have a first-rate play.
   Hear the bells ring, "Ting-a-ling-ding!"
   Hurrah for Thanksgiving Day!

   Over the river and through the wood,
   Trot fast, my dapple-gray!
   Spring over the ground Like a hunting hound!
   For this is Thanksgiving Day.

3. Over the river and through the wood,
   And straight through the barnyard gate.
   We seem to go— Extremely slow
   It is so hard to wait!

   Over the river and through the wood—
   Now Grandmother's cap I spy!
   Hurrah for the fun! Is the pudding done?
   Hurrah for the pumpkin pie!